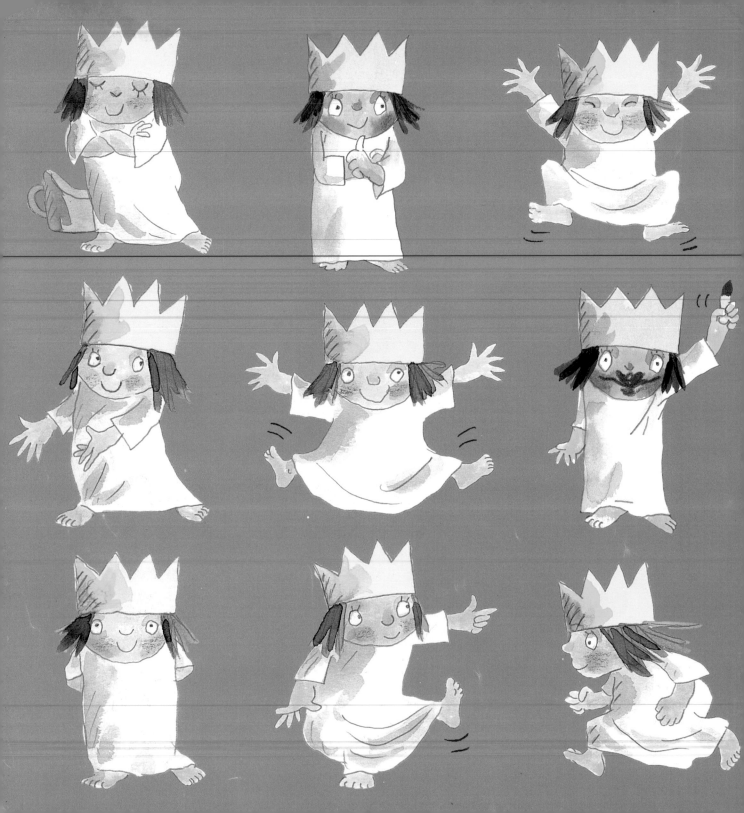

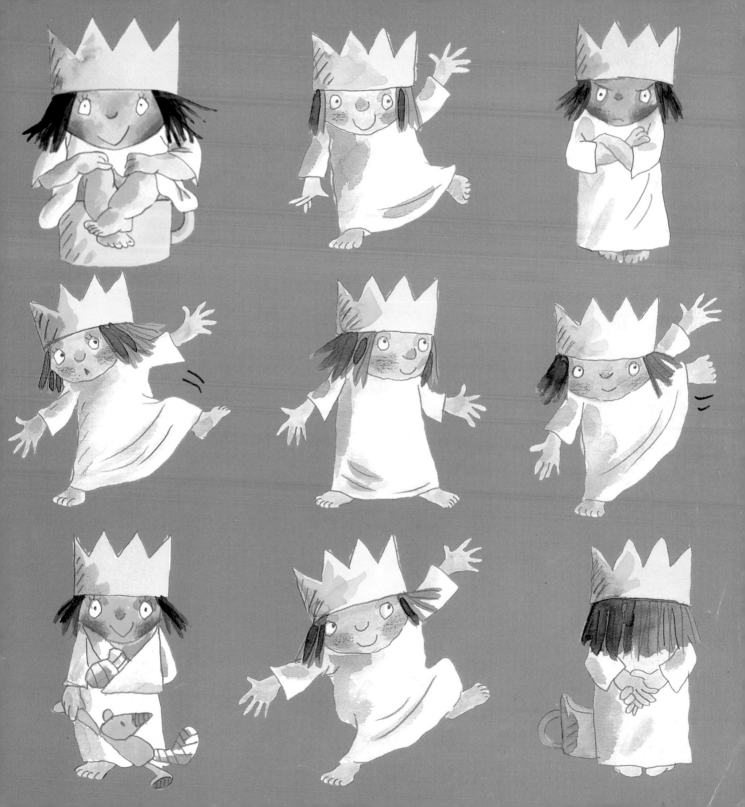

First published in hardback in Great Britain by Andersen Press Ltd in 2003
First published in paperback by Collins Picture Books in 2005

3 5 7 9 10 8 6 4 2

ISBN: 0-00-719478-1

HarperCollins Children's Books is a division of HarperCollins Publishers Ltd.

Text and illustrations copyright © Tony Ross 2003

The author/illustrator asserts the moral right to be identified as the author/illustrator of the work.

A CIP catalogue record for this title is available from the British Library.

Visit our website at: www.harpercollinschildrensbooks.co.uk

Printed and bound in Hong Kong

I Don't Want To Go To Bed

Tony Ross

HarperCollins *Children's Books*

"Why do I have to go to bed when I'm not tired,
and get up when I am?" said the Little Princess.

"I don't WANT to go to bed!" she said.

"Bed is good for you," said the Doctor,
taking her upstairs. "Sleep is even better."

But the Little Princess came straight down again.
"I DON'T WANT TO GO TO BED!" she said.

"I WANT A GLASS OF WATER!"

"There you are," said the Queen.
"Sleepy, sleepy tighty."

"DAAAAAD!"

"You don't want another glass of water?" said the King.
"No," said the Little Princess. "Gilbert does."

"Nighty, nighty," said the King. "Sleepy tighty, Gilbert."
"Don't go!" said the Little Princess. "There's a monster
in the wardrobe."

"There's no such thing as monsters, and there are none in the wardrobe," said the King, closing the bedroom door.

"Dad!" shouted the Little Princess.
"What is it now?" said the King. "You're not still
frightened of monsters?"

"Of course I'm not," said the Little Princess.
"Gilbert is. He says there's one under the bed."

"No there isn't," said the King, creeping out of the bedroom. "There are no such things."

"Stop her!" shouted the Queen. "She's escaped."
"I DON'T WANT TO GO TO BED!" said the Little Princess.
"Why?" said the Queen.

"There's a spider over my bed . . .
. . . and it's got hairy legs."

"Daddy's got hairy legs, and he's nice," said the Queen.

At last the Little Princess went to bed.

Later, when the King went in to kiss her
goodnight, her bed was empty.

Everybody hunted high . . .

. . . and low, until . . .

"Here she is," said the Maid. "She's keeping Gilbert and the cat safe from spiders and monsters."

The next morning, the Little Princess got up
and yawned a yawn. "I'm tired," she said . . .

"I want to go to bed."

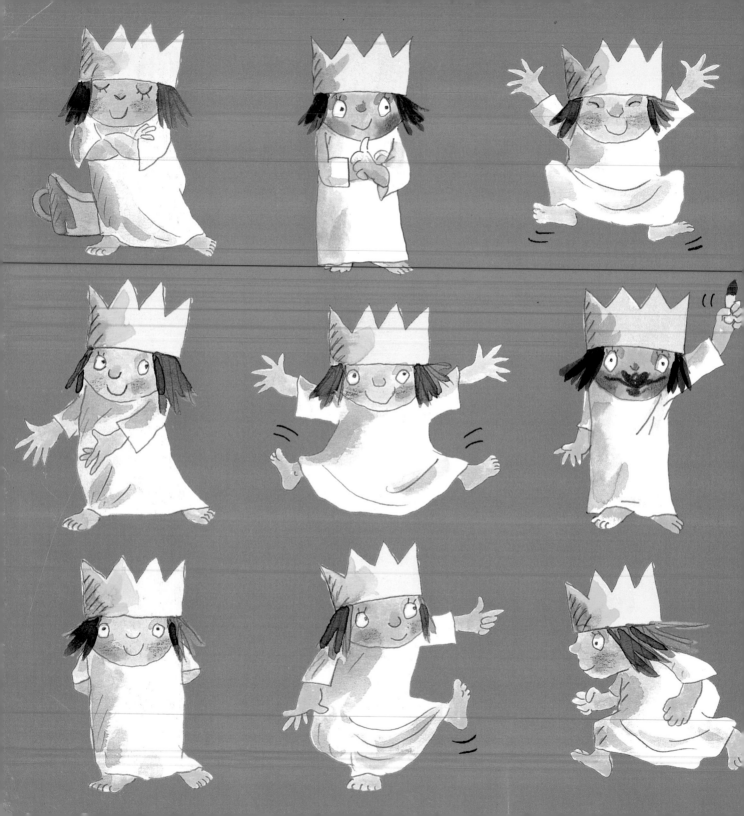

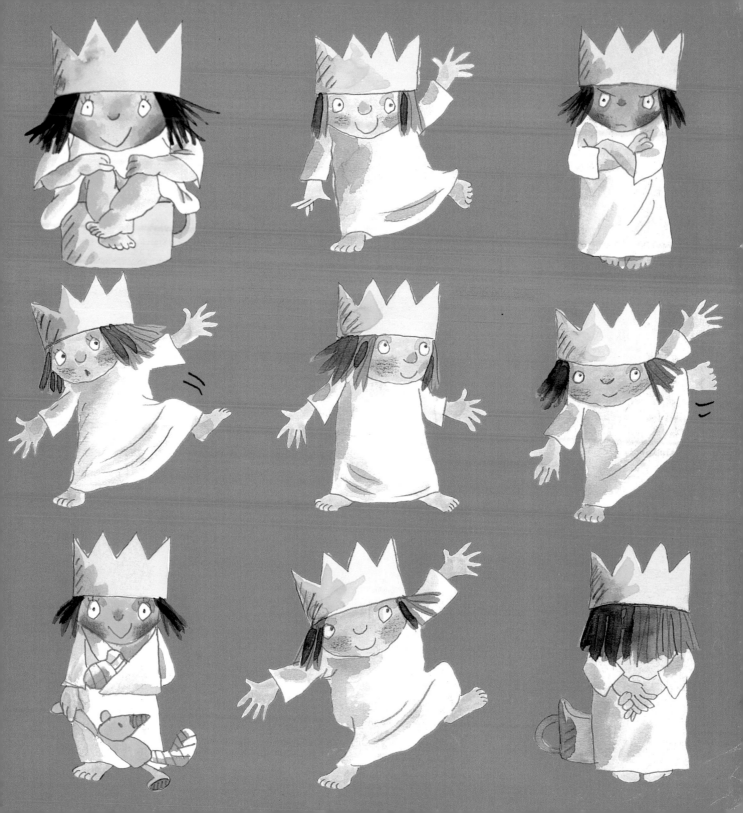

Collect all the funny stories featuring the demanding Little Princess!

0-00-662687-4 — I Want My Potty — Tony Ross

0-00-664357-4 — I Want To Be — Tony Ross

0-00-664356-6 — I Want My Dinner — Tony Ross

0-00-664730-8 — I Want A Sister — Tony Ross

0-00-710957-1 — I Don't Want To Go To Hospital — Tony Ross

0-00-712298-5 — I Want My Dummy — Tony Ross

0-00-715072-5 — I Don't Want To Wash My Hands — Tony Ross

0-00-716312-6 — I Want My Tooth — Tony Ross

Tony Ross was born in London in 1938. His dream was to work with horses but instead he went to art college in Liverpool. Since then, Tony has worked as an art director at an advertising agency, a graphic designer, a cartoonist, a teacher and a film maker – as well as illustrating over 250 books! Tony, his wife Zoe and family live in Macclesfield, Cheshire.